# Favorite ★ Things

### KIMBERLY BRUBAKER BRADLEY

illustrated by

### LAURA HULISKA-BEITH

**Dial Books for Young Readers**  **New York**

To Matthew, my own boy —K.B.B.

For Mom and Dad, suppliers of crayons,
encouragement, and many favorite things
throughout the years. Thank you! —L.H.B.

Published by Dial Books for Young Readers
A division of Penguin Putnam Inc.
345 Hudson Street, New York, New York 10014
Text copyright © 2003 by Kimberly Brubaker Bradley
Pictures copyright © 2003 by Laura Huliska-Beith
All rights reserved
Designed by Lily Malcom. Text set in Beton.
Manufactured in China on acid-free paper
1  3  5  7  9  10  8  6  4  2
Library of Congress Cataloging-in-Publication Data
Bradley, Kimberly Brubaker.
Favorite things / by Kimberly Brubaker Bradley ;
illustrated by Laura Huliska-Beith.
p. cm.
Summary: As his mother tucks him in, Matthew
describes the amazing adventures of his day.
ISBN 0-8037-2597-3
[1 Bedtime—Fiction. 2. Mother and child—Fiction.
3. Imagination—Fiction. 4. Day—Fiction.]
I. Huliska-Beith, Laura, ill. II. Title.
PZ7.B7247 Fav 2003
[E]—dc21      2001028253

The illustrations for this book were done in acrylic,
collaged paper, and fabric on Strathmore paper.

It was bedtime. Daddy read Matthew a story and then Mommy came to kiss him good night.

Mommy turned out the light. She sat on the bed and tucked Matthew's quilt all around him. She gave him three kisses—on his mouth and nose and forehead.

"What was your favorite thing today?" she asked.

Matthew wiggled until his quilt and pillow felt just right. "Hmm," he said. "Maybe it was the elephants that woke me up this morning."

"Elephants!" said Mommy. "I didn't see any elephants."

"You should have heard them," Matthew said. "One had a trumpet in his nose. One had a piano. They sang 'The Star-Spangled Banner.' That's the song everyone sings before a race."

"No wonder you got up so early," said Mommy. "What happened next?"

Matthew shrugged. "The elephants marched down our driveway. They went to Spencer's house to wake *him* up."

Mommy smiled. "Elephants are a good favorite thing."

"But they weren't *my* favorite thing," Matthew said.

"I forgot. My favorite thing was winning the race."

"Which race?" asked Mommy.

"The race to school," Matthew said.

"The one the elephants sang for. Daddy and I had a supersonic car. We took the checkered flag. We got a huge trophy. The elephants went wild."

"Hooray!" said Mommy. "I didn't get any trophies today."

"Maybe you weren't fast enough," said Matthew.

"I guess not," Mommy said. "I got stuck behind a garbage truck."

"Was an elephant driving it?" Matthew asked.

"I didn't notice," Mommy said.

"Well, one of the elephants was driving the race car garbage truck that Dad and I passed," said Matthew. "I'm surprised you didn't see him."

Mommy kissed Matthew again. "If I had won a race, that would have been my favorite too."

"Actually, that wasn't my favorite," said Matthew. "Maybe my favorite was the giant tyrannosaurus squirrel on the playground at school."

"A giant tyrannosaurus squirrel?" said Mommy.

"His name was Rex," Matthew said. "He wasn't afraid of the elephants. He wasn't afraid of *anything*. And he was mean."

"Are you sure?" asked Mommy. "Maybe he was just shy."

"No, because he said, 'Chittle! Chittle! Chittle!' That means: 'Ho! I'm mean, and I'm not afraid of you!' And he was going to capture us, and make us go to his tree castle and count all his acorns."

"Scary," said Mommy.

"I know," said Matthew. "Spencer yelled, 'Go away, Rex!' but I didn't talk to Rex, because you're not supposed to talk to strangers and he was a *really strange* squirrel. So I threw my crackers at him."

"Good thing I put them in your lunch," said Mommy.

"But you didn't put in enough. The elephants got mad, because they love crackers. They said I should have shared.

"And Rex was mad too. He followed us into our classroom."

"No!" said Mommy. "What did Mrs. Burke say about that?"

"She didn't notice," Matthew said. "Spencer had turned into a spider by then and he was hanging from the ceiling. Kristin had extra crackers and she gave some to the elephants, so they weren't mad anymore. I showed Rex my trophy, and he was impressed. He always wanted to meet a race car driver."

"And that," said Mommy, "was your favorite thing."

"No," said Matthew. "But Rex stayed in our classroom all afternoon.

"He painted twenty-four pictures of race cars, and
he gave them all to me. He was very well behaved."
"Was he quiet and still?" asked Mommy.

"He was quieter than the
elephants," said Matthew. "They
had to go in time out."
"And that was your favorite?"
asked Mommy.
"No," said Matthew. "My
favorite wasn't at school."

"Hmm," said Mommy. "Was it the supersonic flying motorcar that picked you up from school?"

"That wasn't a supersonic flying motorcar," Matthew said. "That was you in our regular car."

"Was it having Spencer over to play after school?"

"Spencer didn't come over," Matthew said. "Green Spaceman Spencer did."

"I forgot," Mommy said. "And you were Yellow Spaceman, right?"

"Yellow Spaceman Matthew. We were supersonic superheroes. We saved the planet from all the rude invaders."

"Is that why you were shouting at Emily and Olivia?"

"I wasn't shouting at Emily and Olivia," Matthew said. "Green Spaceman Spencer was—to keep them from invading the planet Wisconsin. That's where all the race car drivers live. And one of the elephants lives in Wisconsin too, and so does Spencer's grandma. But the rest of the elephants come from Ireland."

"Do they wear green?" asked Mommy.

"Of course not," said Matthew. "They wear space suits. How else could they fly?"

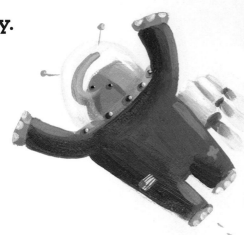

"I thought they were race car drivers," said Mommy.

"Not in Wisconsin," said Matthew.

"But the race car drivers live in Wisconsin," said Mommy.

"Yes, but they don't race there."

"I guess I'm a little confused," said Mommy.

"So was Rex," said Matthew. "But we straightened him out. We were glad he came home with us. Emily and Olivia were afraid of him."

"Was that your favorite thing?" Mommy asked.

"No," said Matthew. "Guess."

"Was it the striped rutabagas we had for supper?"
said Mommy.

"We didn't have striped rutabagas," said Matthew.
"You're making that up."

"Was it the bath Daddy gave you?"
Matthew sighed. "That wasn't a
bath. It was a water race. Spencer
and I raced Emily and Olivia in our
supersonic speedboats, and Rex
made sure all the sharks stayed in
the tugboat."

"I heard a lot of splashing," Mommy said.

"There usually is when you have a race that big. I won."

"I'm not surprised," said Mommy.

"I let Rex take home the trophy," Matthew said. "Then the elephants flew down and scooped up Emily and Olivia and Spencer, and took them home and tucked them into bed. And when the water went out of the tub, all the sharks went down the drain . . .

"But it wasn't my favorite."

Mommy squeezed the end of Matthew's nose. "I don't think you have a favorite thing tonight," she said.

"Yes, I do," Matthew said. "It's a special supersonic secret."

"Does it have anything to do with pirate ships?" asked Mommy. "Or dancing hippopotamuses?"

"It's not any kind of hippopotamus," said Matthew.

Mommy leaned closer. "Tell me," she said.

Matthew put his arms around Mommy's neck and hugged her.

Mommy put her arms around Matthew and hugged him back.

"This," Matthew whispered. "This right now is my favorite thing."

Mommy hugged him tighter. "It's my favorite too," she said.

"The hippopotamuses,"
said Matthew, "are coming
in the morning."